This igloo book belongs to:

....

igloobooks

Published in 2022
First published in the UK by Igloo Books Ltd
An imprint of Igloo Books Ltd
Cottage Farm, NN6 0BJ, UK
Owned by Bonnier Books
Sveavägen 56, Stockholm, Sweden
www.igloobooks.com

1122 002
2 4 6 8 10 9 7 5 3
ISBN 978-1-80022-674-6

Written by Stephanie Moss
Illustrated by Kathryn Inkson

Designed by Hannah George
Edited by Hannah Campling

Printed and manufactured in China

I Love You, Daddy

igloobooks

The morning birds wake us together at dawn.
"Daddy, I love you," I sleepily yawn.

We giggle and splash as we play in the pool.
I love that my friends think my daddy's so cool!

You show me new things
everywhere that we go.
I think you're the cleverest
daddy I know!

If I prick my paw
and I'm starting to cry,
you say, "There, there, little one.
I'll dry your eyes."

We leap in the air and we roll on the ground.
You're the best daddy and best friend around.

I love the adventures we go on together.
I'll always remember them, now and forever.

My legs are too little
to run at your pace.
Until I get faster,
we'll tumble and chase.

I nip at your ears but you don't really mind.
You just smile and laugh. You're always so kind!

I love you, Daddy.
You're brave and strong, too.
I can't wait to grow up
to be just like you!

We cuddle up close
as the stars twinkle bright.
I'll never stop loving you, Daddy.
Goodnight!